LITTLE LIBRARY NUMBER FOUR

TOM CREAN

JOHN & FATTI BURKE

GILL BOOKS

Tom was one of ten children who grew up on a farm near Anascaul in County Kerry.

He loved adventure so much that, at the age of fifteen, he ran away to join the British Navy and sail around the world.

While his ship was moored in New Zealand, Tom met Captain Robert Scott.

Scott's dream was to be the first person ever to reach the South Pole, and he asked Tom to join his crew.

In 1902, after seventeen days' sailing, their ship, *Discovery*, reached Antarctica. But when they made camp in February, the seas froze around them and the ship was trapped.

They lived in the freezing cold for two years, eating seals and seagulls to survive. They even played football on the ice.

Eventually, the ice melted and *Discovery* was able to sail away.

Many years later, Captain Scott organised another expedition with the ship *Terra Nova*. This time they brought dogs and ponies with them to pull their supplies.

Tom loved working with the animals. He even smuggled a rabbit on board!

On Christmas Day, to Tom's surprise, his pet rabbit had seventeen babies. So he gave them to the crew as presents.

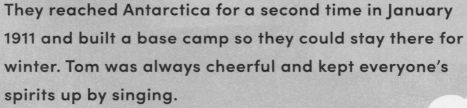

They reached Antarctica for a second time in January 1911 and built a base camp so they could stay there for winter. Tom was always cheerful and kept everyone's spirits up by singing.

As soon as the worst of the weather was over, they were keen to get started. They knew that Roald Amundsen, the famous explorer from Norway, was also trying to be the first to reach the pole. The race was on!

meanwhile...

Sadly, the ponies died from cold and exhaustion, so the men had to haul the sledges themselves. Tom was very strong and tough and always did more than his share.

When they had trekked 1,200 kilometres (the distance from Dublin to Cologne in Germany!), Scott chose just four men to go on the last part of the expedition with him. Tom and his friends Bill Lashly and Teddy Evans weren't chosen, so they had to turn around and head back to Base Camp disappointed.

On the way back, Teddy got very sick, so Tom and Bill pulled him on a sledge. When they could go on no more, they put up a tent and Tom went on alone to get help. He trudged a further 56 kilometres to Hut Point where there were two men with food and supplies. His walk had taken eighteen hours and, thanks to Tom's bravery, Bill and Teddy were saved.

They all waited at Base Camp for Scott to return,
but he never did. All of his party had died and Roald
Amundsen had reached the pole before them.

The Irish explorer Ernest Shackleton wanted to cross Antarctica from coast to coast, and he asked Tom to join him. Tom agreed and in August 1914 they headed south.

This time they went on a ship called *Endurance* – a very fitting name considering what followed! They sailed to South Georgia Island and from there they reached Antarctica, but very soon their ship was trapped in the ice. Not again, thought Tom.

The crew slept on the ship and played games on the ice. One of the dogs they brought even had four puppies!

But after nine months, the ship started to break up. They quickly removed their supplies and three lifeboats before it sank.

The ice was cracking and drifting out to sea. Stranded, they had to find land! They rowed the lifeboats to Elephant Island, a barren rock, where they turned them upside down and sheltered underneath.

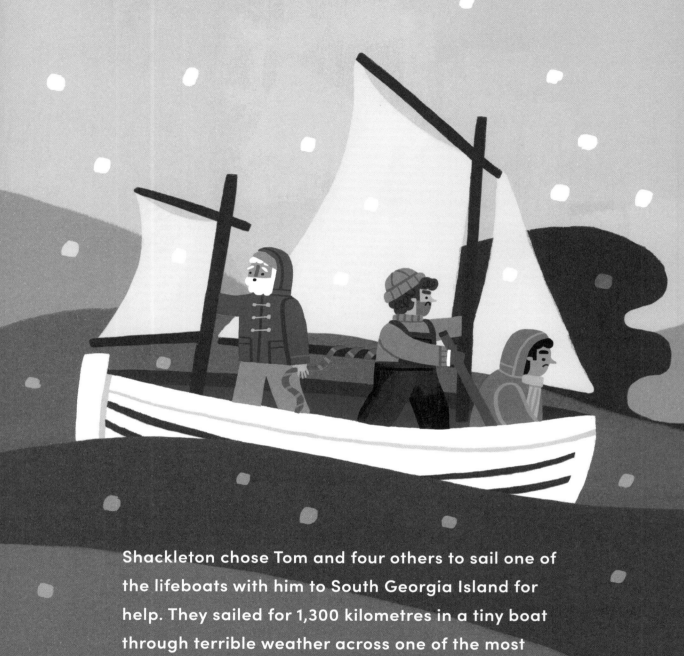

Shackleton chose Tom and four others to sail one of the lifeboats with him to South Georgia Island for help. They sailed for 1,300 kilometres in a tiny boat through terrible weather across one of the most dangerous stretches of water in the world.

Eventually, they came ashore in a damaged boat on the wrong side of the island.

Three of the men were very sick, so Tom, Shackleton and Frank Worsley made the journey of their lives. They walked 64 kilometres across mountains in freezing fog. After 36 hours, they slid down the last mountain at terrific speed and reached the town of Stromness.

The people of the town could not believe that these heroes were still alive. Their sick companions were rescued the next day, but it took a further four months to reach the rest of the men on Elephant Island. Remarkably, they all survived.

After a lifetime of epic adventures, Tom went home to Anascaul. He and his wife Nell opened a pub called the South Pole Inn. It is still there today.

TOM CREAN

His neighbours called him 'Tom the Pole', but he didn't talk of his great adventures or difficulties in Antarctica. Many years after his death Tom became known and celebrated as a hero because of the bravery and kindness he showed his fellow men.

Timeline

1877
Tom is born to Patrick and Catherine Crean.

1893
He leaves home and joins the Royal Navy.

1904
Discovery leaves Antarctica.

1902
He lands in Antarctica on the ship *Discovery* with Captain Robert Scott.

1910
Tom sails with Scott on the *Terra Nova* to Antarctica.

1912
Tom returns to Base Camp with Lashly and Evans. Scott and his expedition party die.

1913
Tom receives the Albert Medal for gallantry.

1917
Tom marries Ellen (Nell) Herlihy.

1916
The adventure to reach Stromness in South Georgia begins.

1920
Tom retires from the Navy.

1915
Endurance is crushed by the ice.

1927
Tom and Nell open the South Pole Inn in Anascaul.

1914
Tom joins Ernest Shackleton's *Endurance* expedition.

1938
Tom dies aged 61.

Did You Know?

Tom received the ALBERT MEDAL, the ROYAL GEOGRAPHICAL MEDAL and THREE POLAR MEDALS for his service and bravery on the *Discovery*, *Terra Nova* and *Endurance* expeditions.

There is a mountain in Antarctica named after Tom. MOUNT CREAN is 2,550 METRES HIGH. It is more than twice the height of Carrauntoohil, Ireland's highest mountain.

When Tom did his solo 56-KILOMETRE WALK to get help for Lieutenant Teddy Evans, his only food consisted of THREE BISCUITS and TWO STICKS OF CHOCOLATE.

CREAN GLACIER is also named after Tom. It is 4 MILES LONG and on the north coast of SOUTH GEORGIA.

The crew mainly ate what was known as 'HOOSH': a thick stew made from PEMMICAN (a mixture of fat, dried meat and cereal), thickened with crushed ship's BISCUITS and BOILING WATER.

When Tom went back to the ROYAL NAVY after his adventures, he was stationed at Chatham, Cobh and Berehaven. He rose to the rank of WARRANT OFFICER (as a boatswain) before he retired in 1920.

Tom and Nell had three daughters, MARY, KATE and EILEEN. Sadly, Kate died aged four.

When a major exhibition about Tom opened in 2002, EDMUND HILLARY, the first person to climb Mount Everest, payed tribute to Tom, saying, 'He was a great man of IMMENSE STRENGTH and ENDURANCE and afraid of very little.' Tom's daughters and Teddy Evans' son were also present.

In July 2003 a BRONZE STATUE of Tom was unveiled across from his pub in Anascaul. The pub is still in operation and contains a collection of Tom Crean memorabilia.

The Dingle Brewing Company in Kerry produce a drink called TOM CREAN LAGER, named in his honour.

TOM'S SINGING kept the crew's spirits up during tough times. SHACKLETON wrote of Tom's singing, 'He always sang when he was steering, and nobody ever discovered what the song was ... but somehow it was CHEERFUL.'

ABOUT the AUTHORS

KATHI 'FATTI' BURKE is
an illustrator from County
Waterford.

JOHN BURKE is Fatti's dad.
He is a retired primary school
teacher and principal.

Their first book, *Irelandopedia*, won *The Ryan Tubridy Show*
Listeners' Choice Award at the Irish Book Awards 2015, and the
Eilís Dillon Award for first children's book and the Judges' Special
Award at the CBI Book of the Year Awards 2016. Their next
books, *Historopedia* and *Foclóiropedia*, were nominated for the
Specsavers Children's Book of the Year (Junior) Award at the Irish
Book Awards 2016 and 2017. Their books have sold over 100,000
copies in Ireland.

ALSO in the LITTLE LIBRARY SERIES

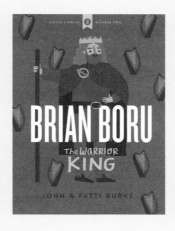

BOOK ONE　　　　**BOOK TWO**　　　　**BOOK THREE**

ALSO by the AUTHORS

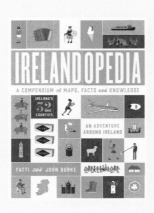

Gill Books
Hume Avenue
Park West
Dublin 12
www.gillbooks.ie

Gill Books is an imprint of M.H. Gill and Co.

Text © John Burke 2020
Illustrations © Kathi Burke 2020
978 07171 8656 3

Designed by www.grahamthew.com
L&C Printing Group, Poland

This book is typeset in 13pt on 25pt Sofia Pro.

The paper used in this book comes from the wood pulp of managed forests. For every tree felled, at least one tree is planted, thereby renewing natural resources.

A CIP catalogue record for this book is available from the British Library.

5 4 3 2